PRANK ACADEMY...

WELCOME TO PRANK ACADEMY ....

SCHOOL RULES ....

PERFECT PRANKS 8

CATEGORIES 10

GUIDANCE 11

THE PRANKS... 13

     1.SMALL SHOES 16

     2.SALT AND SUGAR SWITCHEROO 17

     3.WHOOPPEE CUSHION WHOOPSIE 18

     4. MMM YUMMY FLIES 19

     5. TICK TOCK 20

     6. INTO THE UNKNOWN 21

     7. WARDROBE MADNESS..................................22

     8. WATER VOLCANO 23

     9. BATTERY BANDIT 25

     10. NICE OR SPICE 26

     11. WAITER THERE'S A WORM IN MY SOUP 27

     12. JACK IN THE BOX 28

     14. RUBBER BAND-IT 31

     15. TOILET ROLL TWOOSIE 32

     16. SALT WATER SWIG 33

     17. BROWNIE OR BROWN E 34

     18. THERE'S A SNAKE IN MY BOOT 35

     19. CRISPY CREAM 36

     20. TOILET ROLL TAMPER 38

     21. WET NECK SNEEZERONI 40

     22. EGGCELLENT IDEA 1 41

     23. QUESTIONABLE SQUASH.............................42

     24. TERRIFYING TOILET ROLL 43

25. OREO SURPRISE 44

26. SHAMPOO SABOTAGE 45

27. WHAT'S THAT SCARY BEAST... 46

28. COLACANO 48

29. SINK SABOTAGE 49

30. CEREAL SURPRISE 50

31. BUBBLE BED 51

32. CLOTHING CALAMITY 52

33. WEIRD WALLPAPER 53

34. PRINGLE PRANK 54

35. PEN CAP CAPER 56

36. ALARM CLOCK CHAOS 57

37. IT NEVER RAINS IT POURS 58

38. TOILET ROLL TOMFOOLERY 59

39. TOILET TERRORS 60

40. VARNISH VANDAL 61

41. BALLOON LAMPOON 63

42. SPONGE CAKE??? 64

43. FAMILY FORTUNES 66

44. AMAZING APPLE 68

45. CARWASH CAPERS 70

46. JELLY JOKES 71

47. WATER BOTTLE WOE 72

48. SHAVING FOAM SHENANIGANS 73

49. SUPER SPAM 74

50. UPSIDE DOWN DAFTNESS 75

51. WATERFALL 76

52. PHONE FROLIC 78

53. DOOR DECEPTION 80

54. PENNY PUZZLE 82

55. MASH MADNESS 83

56. EGGCELLENT IDEA 2 85

57. WATER BOTTLE WASH 86

58. BALANCING ACT 87

59. WHY DOES MY SOAP SMELL LIKE CHEESE 88

60. COOKIE MONSTER 89

GRADUATION **90**

PRANK ACADEMY

Practical jokes for kids of all ages

- BY CLINT HAMMERSTRIKE

WELCOME TO PRANK ACADEMY

Welcome to the Prank Academy, the school for practical jokes. I am your Headmaster Clint Hammerstrike and I will be teaching you how to pull hilarious pranks on your unsuspecting friends and family.

At Prank Academy you are going to learn how to create mischief, make people laugh and create fantastic surprises.

Some of these pranks are quick and require little or no materials to complete. Others will require some items and forward planning to successfully pull off. With a wide range of pranks there should be a prank to catch anyone out.

SCHOOL RULES

To ensure that pranks are fun for everyone, don't hurt anyone or damage anything Prank Academy has a few key rules:

RULE 1: DON'T BE MEAN

A great practical joke is meant to be funny – not just for you but the person being surprised. Do not play pranks on people that won't enjoy it or might already be upset. The aim is to make people laugh not cry.

RULE 2: ONLY PRANK PEOPLE YOU KNOW

Pranks are best when they are played on people you know, so you can laugh with them about it later. There is no way of knowing how a stranger will react.

RULE 3: ALWAYS CLEAN UP YOUR MESS

Pranks can be messy, help clean them up afterwards. Think ahead about what you might need to clean up after your prank.

RULE 4: DON'T SPOIL SOMETHING THAT ISN'T YOURS

Be careful that you don't damage or break something that doesn't belong to you? Make sure you undertake pranks in a safe and suitable place. Don't do silly things like spill water on electrical items like TVs, laptops or phones. If in doubt ask an adult.

RULE 5: BE A GOOD SPORT

If you pull pranks on other people you must accept that other people might prank you back. Make sure you react well to being pranked and enjoy the surprise.

PERFECT PRANKS

To help you pull of your prank perfectly below are some tips to keep in mind:

PREPARATION

Make sure that you read through all the steps of the prank and think through how you will deliver the prank. Ensure you have all the right material. If necessary, do a test first.

KEEP A STRAIGHT FACE

It's important when pulling a prank that the target doesn't know what's coming. Make sure you don't start laughing or making funny faces as this might give you away.

ACT NORMAL

Act as normal as possible so that you don't tip them off. Make sure you don't stare at your target or where your prank might be hidden.

SPREAD PRANKS OUT FOR MAXIMUM EFFECT

In order to ensure that your pranks work and stay funny make sure to spread your pranks out. You don't want to do loads of prank on the same day on the same targets as they will be expecting them.

CATEGORIES

The pranks in this book have been organised into three categories

EASY ENTERTAINMENT

Pranks in this category are quick and simple to deliver with little preparation or material.

MEDIUM MISCHIEF

Pranks in this category require a little preparation and some materials.

HILARIOUSLY HARD

Pranks in this category will require preparation, and may take longer to deliver – worth it for how funny the results will be.

GUIDANCE

Some pranks in this book are labelled with symbols. These symbols are to help ensure the pranks you play are safe for you and your target. Following these symbols will help you have fun and make sure nothing goes wrong.

ASK AN ADULT

Some of the pranks in this book might require an adult to help you with preparation if you are young – such as using scissors to cut or make holes, climb ladders or use ovens. Where you see the **ASK AN ADULT** symbol ask an adult to help assist you. Your adult helper will be your teaching assistant at Prank Academy and will help you deliver the prank safely.

ALLERGY WARNING Some of the pranks in this book require your target to eat food. Where you see the **ALLERGY WARNING** symbol check with an adult to make sure that there are no ingredients in the prank that might be harmful to your target. If in doubt play this prank on a different target.

Some of the pranks in this books can get a bit messy. Where you see the **MESSY** symbol make sure you do not perform this prank near electronics, valuable items or furniture that might be stained. Be prepared to help clear up afterward. Some of these pranks might be best played outside or in a non-carpeted room.

THE PRANKS

As your headmaster at Prank Academy for each prank I will be teaching you everything you need to know to pull it off. For each prank I will set out all the materials that you need to collect. I will then give you a step-by-step guide on how to deliver the prank.

For each prank there is also a box like the one below:

When you have successfully completed this prank you can tick this box so that you know you have played this prank and can move onto your next class.

Complete all the pranks in this book and you will have graduated from Prank Academy with qualifications in mischief and mayhem.

So let's get onto the pranks.......

EASY ENTERTAINMENT

1.SMALL SHOES

Pull this prank off and you will have your target wondering whether their feet have grown or their shoes have shrunk

PRANK RATING: Easy Entertainment

MATERIALS:

- ❖ Your targets shoes
- ❖ A pair of socks

PRANK PREPARATION:

- ⌘ Step 1: When your target isn't looking grab their shoes.
- ⌘ Step 2: Take the pair of socks. Roll up each sock and push it right to the end of your targets shoe. Repeat for the other shoe.
- ⌘ Step 3: Sit back and watch your target get confused as they discover their shoes no longer fit.

2.SALT AND SUGAR SWITCHEROO

Pull this prank off at the dinner table and when your target thinks they are salting their potatoes they will really be turning them into "sweet" potatoes!

PRANK RATING: Easy Entertainment

ALLERGY WARNING

MATERIALS:

❖ Salt Shaker – The pouring kind rather than the grinding kind.

❖ White Sugar

PRANK PREPARATION:

⌘ Step 1: Before dinner find the salt shaker

⌘ Step 2: Pour out the salt and fill this back up with white sugar.

⌘ Step 3: Place the salt shaker back on the table.

⌘ Step 4: Sit back and wait for someone to reach for the salt. Make sure you don't laugh!

3.WHOOPPEE CUSHION WHOOPSIE

Pull this prank off and you will have completed a timeless classic. Just wait for your target to sit down and let rip!

PRANK RATING: Easy Entertainment

MATERIALS:

❖ Whoopee Cushion

❖ A seat – armchair or sofa with a cushion.

PRANK PREPARATION:

⌘ Step 1: Inflate the whoopee cushion in advance. You don't want your target to hear you blowing it up.

⌘ Step 2: Wait till your target leaves the room. Place the whoopee cushion under their seat making sure the whoopee cushion isn't visible. If the person just got up from the seat, make sure it looks the same when they return.

⌘ Step 3: Sit down and act natural until your target sits on the whoopee cushion and lets out a champion fart!

4. MMM YUMMY FLIES

Pull this prank off and get your target's tummy turning. What could be more delicious that eating a juicy fly!

PRANK RATING: Easy Entertainment

MATERIALS:

❖ A tissue

❖ A raisin or sultana

PRANK PREPARATION:

⌘ Step 1: Pretend that there is an annoying fly buzzing around the house. It works even better if there is an actual one buzzing about!

⌘ Step 2: Take a tissue and pretend that you have caught and squashed the fly in the tissue. Really you just have just placed a squashed raisin or sultana in there.

⌘ Step 3: Show your target a quick flash of the tissue so they see something dark in the tissue – they will think it's a fly.

⌘ Step 4: Without them seeing any more eat the raisin straight off the tissue and pull a yummy in my tummy face!

5. TICK TOCK

Pull this prank off and have everyone in the house panicking that they are running late with this simple but dastardly prank.

PRANK RATING: Easy Entertainment

MATERIALS:

- ❖ A clock
- ❖ A step ladder or chair for reaching high-up clocks.

PRANK PREPARATION:

⌘ Step 1: For clocks with hands simply wind the long minute hand forward one hour.

⌘ Step 2: For digital clocks use the buttons on the back of the clock to add one hour onto the digital screen.

⌘ Step 3: Have patience this prank may take a while to land. But just wait for the chaos to happen when your target thinks they are running 1 hour late.

6. INTO THE UNKNOWN

Pull this prank off and you could have your target thinking that their room has been invaded by a swarm of bees, a dinosaur or perhaps a scary ghost.

PRANK RATING: Easy Entertainment

MATERIALS:

❖ Two mobile phones – you may need to borrow them from others in your home.

PRANK PREPARATION:

⌘ Step 1: When your target is out of the room use one of the phones to call the other. Quickly answer the phone and turn it onto speaker mode. Then hide the phone somewhere in the room and then leave.

⌘ Step 2: Wait until your target has entered the room. When they have been in there a little while, you can start making your funny noises.

⌘ Step 3: Enjoy their confusion as they try and work out what on earth is hiding in the room with them.

7. WARDROBE MADNESS

Pull this prank off and you will have your target scratching their heads wondering what they just saw.

PRANK RATING: Easy Entertainment

MATERIALS:

❖ One supercool outfit

PRANK PREPARATION:

⌘ Step 1: Let people see you wearing a normal outfit.

⌘ Step 2: Sneak back to your bedroom and take off all your clothes and put them on back to front

⌘ Step 3: Walk back in with people and pretend like nothing has changed.

⌘ Step 4: Keep alternating between wearing clothes the right way round and back to front and wait for people to start getting confused.

8. WATER VOLCANO

Pull this prank off and you will have your target going from confusion to shock as they get a soaking surprise.

PRANK RATING: *Easy Entertainment*

MESSY

MATERIALS:

❖ One squeezable plastic water bottle with cap off

❖ Water

❖ A coin

PRANK PREPARATION:

⌘ Step 1: Fill the bottle up to just below the rim with water.

⌘ Step 2: Place the bottle on top of a coin.

⌘ Step 2: Call your target over telling them that there is a coin in your water bottle.

⌘ Step 4: Let them look in the top of the bottle.

⌘ Step 5: When they put their face near the bottle to look inside squeeze the bottle hard causing the water to shoot out the top and soak your target.

⌘ Clean Up: When you stop laughing offer your target a towel and help mop up the mess.

Pull this prank off and whoever hogs the TV remote in your family and always gets to choose the channel will be left fuming when the TV doesn't listen to them.

9. BATTERY BANDIT

Pull this prank off and whoever hogs the TV remote in your family and always gets to choose the channel will be left fuming when the TV doesn't listen to them.

PRANK RATING: Easy Entertainment

MATERIALS:

❖ TV Remote

PRANK PREPARATION:

⌘ Step 1: Wait till your target is watching a programme

⌘ Step 2: When they leave the room grab the remote and either turn off the TV or pause it. If they have already paused the TV skip this step and go straight to step 3.

⌘ Step 3: Take the batteries out the back of the remote and hide them out of sight.

⌘ Step 4: Leave the room before they come back in and listen as realise can't restart watching their programme.

10. NICE OR SPICE

Pull this prank off and you will give your target a delicious treat that turns into a spicy nightmare.

PRANK RATING: Easy Entertainment

MATERIALS:

ALLERGY WARNING

- ❖ 1 pack of regular Jelly Beans
- ❖ 1 pack of Jelly Belly Hot Cinnamon Flavour – Available on Amazon.

PRANK PREPARATION:

⌘ Step 1: Offer your target a jelly bean from the ordinary jelly bean bag. Let them eat it and enjoy it.

⌘ Step 2: Casually leave the room and empty out the regular jelly beans out of their bag into a bowl.

⌘ Step 3: Pour the Hot Cinnamon jelly beans into the regular Jelly Bean bag

⌘ Step 4: Go back into the room and offer your target another Jelly Bean. This time instead of a sweet treat they will get a spicy surprise.

11. WAITER THERE'S A WORM IN MY SOUP

Pull this prank off and you will have your target throwing up in their plate as they discover a wriggly worm in their dinner.

PRANK RATING: Easy Entertainment

MATERIALS:

❖ A bag of jelly worms or gummy snakes.

PRANK PREPARATION:

⌘ Step 1: Help dish up dinner

⌘ Step 2: Sneak your jelly worm into your targets food – it doesn't have to be soup (mash potato works well).

⌘ Step 3: Take the plate of food through to your target and make sure not to give anything away.

⌘ Step 4: Sit down and tuck into your dinner and wait for your target to discover a worm in their food.

12. JACK IN THE BOX

Pull this prank off and you will have completed another classic surprise prank, guaranteed to give your target a hilarious fright.

PRANK RATING: Easy Entertainment

MATERIALS:

- ❖ A cardboard box big enough to fit in
- ❖ A pair of scissors

PRANK PREPARATION:

⌘ Step 1: With the scissors make a very small hole in the side of the box so that you can see out. Climb into the box.

⌘ Step 2: Climb into the box. Ask someone to help you close the flaps up.

⌘ Step 3: Peeking through the small hole wait for your target to come into the room and get comfortable. Stay as quiet and still as possible.

⌘ Step 4: When they have settled down jump out of the box with a big shout!

⌘ Alternative – If you do not have a large cardboard box try using a suitcase. Instead of cutting a hole in the suitcase leave the zip undone so that you can still see and jump out to surprise your target.

13. CEREAL PRANKSTER

Pull this prank off and enjoy the look on your targets face when they go to pour out their Cheerios and they end up with a bowl of cornflakes!

PRANK RATING: Easy Entertainment

MATERIALS:

❖ Two open boxes of cereal.

ALLERGY
WARNING

PRANK PREPARATION:

⌘ Step 1: When your target isn't in the kitchen take the cereal bags out of two different open cereal boxes.

⌘ Step 2: Switch the cereal bags into the other box i.e. Cheerio bag into the Cornflakes box.

⌘ Step 3: Wait for your target to pour out their morning cereal and watch the confusion spread.

14. RUBBER BAND-IT

Pull off this prank and when your target rushes to see who is calling they will find a most irritating surprise waiting for them.

PRANK RATING: Easy Entertainment

MATERIALS:

❖ Lots or rubber bands

❖ A phone

PRANK PREPARATION:

⌘ Step 1: When your target leaves their phone unattended grab the rubber bands and stretch as many rubber bands over the phone as possible. Try and criss-cross the rubber bands covering the whole screen.

⌘ Step 2: Using another phone call the targets phone. When they rush in to answer the phone they won't be able to answer the phone – don't let them see that it is you calling.

⌘ Step 3: Before they finish unwrapping the phone hang-up.

⌘ Step 4: Watch their frustration.

15. TOILET ROLL TWOOSIE

Honestly can you beat a poop prank? Pull this prank off and your target will be disgusted when they find your perfectly handcrafted poop!

PRANK RATING: Easy Entertainment

MATERIALS:

❖ Two used toilet roll tube

❖ A bowl of water

PRANK PREPARATION:

⌘ Step 1: Take the cardboard toilet roll tube and tear this into small pieces

⌘ Step 2: Soak the pieces in water and squash the pieces together, rolling it into the shape of a poo.

⌘ Step 3: Leave this in a funny place – i.e. a shoe, on the kitchen floor, in the bath or on your targets pillow.

⌘ Step 4: Wait for your target to discover the poop!

16. SALT WATER SWIG

Pull this prank off and when your target goes to take a big swig of water they will end up drinking the ocean instead.

PRANK RATING: Easy Entertainment

MATERIALS:

❖ Salt

❖ A teaspoon

❖ A glass of water

PRANK PREPARATION:

⌘ Step 1: When you are about to eat dinner together at the table offer to help set the table and get the drinks.

⌘ Step 2: Make the drinks for your family normally, accept for your targets. For their drink put in three teaspoons of salt and stir until the salt dissolves.

⌘ Step 4: Put the drinks on the table making sure you remember which one is your targets drink.

⌘ Step 5: Wait for them to take a swig and discover they just got salted!

17. BROWNIE OR BROWN E

Pull this prank off and your target is going to extremely disappointed when a tasty treat turns into cardboard misery.

PRANK RATING: *Easy Entertainment*

MATERIALS:

- ❖ A brown cardboard box
- ❖ A pair of scissors
- ❖ A plate

PRANK PREPARATION:

⌘ Step 1: Using scissors cut a large capital E out of brown cardboard. Aim for one about 10cm high by 4cm wide.

⌘ Step 2: Ask your target if they would like a freshly made brownie.

⌘ Step 3: When they say yes, leave the room and get your Brown E, put this on a plate and then bring it back into the room.

⌘ Step 4: Tell them, here is your Brown E!

18. THERE'S A SNAKE IN MY BOOT

Pull this prank off and when your target is hurrying to put their shoes on they will find this terrifying beast instead.

PRANK RATING: Easy Entertainment

MATERIALS:

❖ A scary toy animal – snake, spider etc.

❖ Your targets shoes

PRANK PREPARATION:

⌘ Step 1: Locate your targets shoes.

⌘ Step 2: Hide the scary animal toy in their shoe.

⌘ Step 3: Wait for them to try and put their shoe on. When your target attempts to put their shoe on they are going to get a fright when they find the little beasty!

19. CRISPY CREAM

Pull this prank off and when your target reaches for a delicious handful of crunchy crisps they are instead going to be met with a sloppy mess.

PRANK RATING: Easy Entertainment

MATERIALS:

❖ A big share bag of crisps

❖ A can of spray cream

MESSY

ALLERGY WARNING

PRANK PREPARATION:

⌘ Step 1: Take a big family bag of crisps – make sure it's a flavour your target likes. Empty the crisps out into a bowl.

⌘ Step 2: Take a can of spray cream and half fill the bag with cream. Sprinkle a couple of crisps over the top so the cream isn't visible.

⌘ Step 3: Walk into the room eating a crisp. Ask your target if they would like one.

⌘ Step 4: Hold the bag out to your target without letting them see into the bag. When they reach into the bag push the bag upwards and squeeze covering their hand in cream!

⌘ Clean Up: Offer your target a cloth to clean up.

20. TOILET ROLL TAMPER

Pull off this prank and when your target goes to wipe up after going to the toilet they are going to be left bamboozled trying to find the end of the toilet roll.

PRANK RATING: Easy Entertainment

MATERIALS:

- ❖ A toilet roll
- ❖ Clear Sellotape
- ❖ A pair of scissors

PRANK PREPARATION:

⌘ Step 1: Sneak into the toilet.

⌘ Step 2: Take your Sellotape and tape across the width of the edge of the toilet roll end. With a pair of scissors cut off any tape that sticks out over the edge.

⌘ Step 3: Wait for your target to go to the toilet and listen out for their frustration when they try and get some toilet paper to wipe their bottom!

MEDIUM MISCHIEF

21. WET NECK SNEEZERONI

Pull off this prank and your target will end up thinking you have just unleashed the wettest slimiest sneeze down the back of their neck.

PRANK RATING: Medium Mischief

MATERIALS:

❖ A clean spray bottle or small water pistol filled with water.

PRANK PREPARATION:

⌘ Step 1: Sneak up behind your target without them knowing you are there.

⌘ Step 2: Let out a fake sneeze noise whilst simultaneously spraying the back of their neck with the water

⌘ Step 3: Quickly hide the water bottle or water pistol so that they think you actually just sneezed on them.

⌘ Step 4: After a few seconds let them know that it was a prank.

22. EGGCELLENT IDEA 1

Pull of this prank and when your target goes to the fridge to get some eggs they are going to be confronted with some terrifying faces staring back at them.

PRANK RATING: Medium Mischief

MATERIALS:

- ❖ A felt tip pen or Sharpie Marker
- ❖ Googly eyes
- ❖ A box of eggs
- ❖ PVA glue

PRANK PREPARATION:

- ⌘ Step 1: Gently remove an egg from the box and using your pen carefully draw a funny face on the egg.
- ⌘ Step 2: Do this for all the eggs. Try and follow a theme for your pictures – maybe a Viking army or ninjas!
- ⌘ Step 4: Use PVA glue to stick on googly eyes for extra impact.
- ⌘ Step 3: Replace eggs and wait.

23. WHAT'S IN MY SQUASH

Pull this prank off and you will leave your target wondering why their favourite drink tastes so bad.

PRANK RATING: Medium Mischief

ALLERGY WARNING

MATERIALS:

❖ Food colouring to match the colour squash or fruit juice your imitating.

❖ A glass filled with drinking water

❖ A spoon

PRANK PREPARATION:

⌘ Step 1: Ask your target if they would like a glass of squash or juice. If they say yes go to the kitchen and do step 2.

⌘ Step 2: Take a glass of water and add in a few drops of food colouring that matches the colour of the squash (i.e. yellow food colouring for orange squash or red colouring for a berry flavour) and mix with a spoon.

⌘ Step 3: Give your target the glass and casually watch their reaction when they take a sip.

24. TERRIFYING TOILET ROLL

Pull off this prank on your target to leave them wondering how the toilet roll knows so much about them or why it is so rude!

PRANK RATING: Medium Mischief

MATERIALS:

❖ A marker pen

❖ Toilet roll

PRANK PREPARATION:

⌘ Step 1: Unroll a couple of layers of toilet roll.

⌘ Step 2: Take your marker and write a message along the toilet roll. Try to write quickly so the paper doesn't blot. You can either write something about the target that most people wouldn't know or it can be something funny like "yuk that really smells".

⌘ Step 3: Roll the toilet roll back up to hide the message, which will only be revealed when your target goes to wipe up after using the toilet.

25. OREO SURPRISE

Pull off this prank and watch your targets face go from drooling to disgust in seconds.

PRANK RATING: Medium Mischief

MATERIALS:

❖ A pack of original Oreo biscuits

❖ A tube of plain white toothpaste.

❖ A spoon

PRANK PREPARATION:

⌘ Step 1: Take an Oreo and carefully twist the two biscuits to separate and open it up.

⌘ Step 2: Using a spoon gently scrape out the Oreo Cream.

⌘ Step 3: Squeeze toothpaste onto one of the biscuits and then place the other biscuit on top.

⌘ Step 4: Place the pranked Oreo back in the packet and offer one to your target or alternatively make 5 or 6 pranked Oreos and leave them out on a plate.

26. SHAMPOO SABOTAGE

Pull this prank off and your target will go red with rage as they try to work out why their shampoo just won't come out. – This prank works for most other bottles i.e. shower gel, tomato sauce and many more.

PRANK RATING: Medium Mischief

MATERIALS:

❖ Sellotape

❖ Your targets bottle of shampoo

PRANK PREPARATION:

⌘ Step 1: Find the bottle that you want to prank.

⌘ Step 2: Unscrew the lid and place the bottle down. Take a piece of Sellotape and stick this inside the cap covering the inside of the hole. Use a couple of pieces to make sure the hole is well and truly sealed.

⌘ Step 3: Screw the lid back on the bottle and wait for your target to take their next shower or bath.

27. WHAT'S THAT SCARY BEAST...

Pull this prank off and terrify your target into thinking that a terrifying bug has crawled into their room.

PRANK RATING: Medium Mischief

MATERIALS:

❖ A piece of paper

❖ A black colouring pen

❖ Sellotape

❖ Scissors

ASK AN ADULT

PRANK PREPARATION:

⌘ Step 1: On a piece of paper draw out a picture of a terrifying insect. Trace one from a book if you can't draw it freehand.

⌘ Step 2: Using scissors cut out your insect and then colour both sides of your insect in black.

⌘ Step 2: Once your picture has dried use Sellotape to stick the insect onto the inside of a lamp shade in a place that will be clearly visible to your target. Make sure that the light is switched off when you do this as the bulb can get very hot.

⌘ Step 3: Keep the light turned off. When your target turns on the light they will get a wicked fright.

28. COLACANO

Pull off this prank and you will turn your target's relaxing glass of cola into a gushing volcano. This prank is best played outside or in the kitchen.

PRANK RATING: *Medium Mischief*

MATERIALS:

❖ A glass of cola

❖ An ice cube tray

❖ A pack of Mentos Sweets

PRANK PREPARATION:

⌘ Step 1: Drop a Mentos sweet into each section of an ice cube try and then fill with water. Place ice cube tray in a freezer for 2 hours.

⌘ Step 2: When the ice cubes have set ask your target whether they would like a nice cold glass of cola. When they say yes pour the cola into a glass and drop in a couple of pranked ice cubes.

⌘ Step 3: When the ice cubes melt the Mentos will react with the cola and cause a cola volcano.

29. SINK SABOTAGE

Pull off this prank and when your target goes to wash their hands they will be soaked in seconds!

PRANK RATING: Medium Mischief

MATERIALS:

- ❖ Sellotape
- ❖ Scissors

ASK AN ADULT

PRANK PREPARATION:

⌘ Step 1: Using scissors cut strips of Sellotape. Use the Sellotape to tape over the bottom of the tap hole. Make sure the Sellotape is securely fixed.

⌘ Step 2: Leave a really small hole facing out towards the sink.

⌘ Step 3: When your target goes to wash their hands the water will spray out of the small opening soaking them.

30. CEREAL SURPRISE

Pull off this prank and shock your target when they sit down to enjoy a nice bowl of cereal.

PRANK RATING: Medium Mischief

MATERIALS:

ALLERGY WARNING

- ❖ A bowl, spoon, cereal and milk
- ❖ Green food colouring

PRANK PREPARATION:

⌘ Step 1: Offer to make your target some cereal for breakfast. Put the milk on the table for them to pour out themselves.

⌘ Step 2: Pour a good splash of green food colouring into the bottom of the bowl.

⌘ Step 3: Cover the food colouring with a layer of cereal.

⌘ Step 4: Bring your target their bowl of cereal. Watch their surprise when they pour the milk into their cereal and the milk starts turning green.

31. BUBBLE BED

Pull off this prank and when your target lies down for a rest they are going to get a loud surprise.

PRANK RATING: Medium Mischief

MATERIALS:

❖ Bubble wrap

PRANK PREPARATION:

⌘ Step 1: When your target is out of their bedroom sneak in and remove their sheet from their bed.

⌘ Step 2: Lay bubble wrap on top of their mattress.

⌘ Step 3: For bonus points slip some bubble wrap into their pillowcase.

⌘ Step 4: Put the sheet back on the bed and make sure you leave the bed looking the same as your target left it.

32. CLOTHING CALAMITY

Pull off this prank and when your target goes to get dressed and find that perfect outfit, they are going to be greeted with a confusing riddle of a wardrobe.

PRANK RATING: Medium Mischief

MATERIALS:

❖ No materials required

PRANK PREPARATION:

⌘ Step 1: When your target is out of their bedroom sneak in and try to reorganise as much of their wardrobe and drawers as possible.

⌘ Step 2: In their wardrobe swap where their clothes are hanging up i.e. move trousers to where dresses or shirts are hanging.

⌘ Step 3: In their drawers if there are identical shape drawers, just switch the position they are in the chest of drawers. If they aren't removable lift out contents of draws and swap with another draw i.e. socks for pants.

33. WEIRD WALLPAPER

Pull off this prank and when your target goes to check their phone they are going to be greeted with a weird and wonderful surprise on their phones wallpaper.

PRANK RATING: Medium Mischief

MATERIALS:

❖ Your targets phone.

PRANK PREPARATION:

⌘ Step 1: Try and get access to your targets phone. Maybe wait until they are having a shower or a bath.

⌘ Step 2: Open up their phone and take a photo of something strange or funny.

⌘ Step 3: Go into their settings and set the photo as their wallpaper. Put the phone back exactly how you found it and wait for them to discover your handy work.

34. PRINGLE PRANK

Pull off this prank and when your target goes to reach for a handful of Pringles all they are going to get is a soaking.

PRANK RATING: Medium Mischief

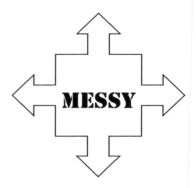

MATERIALS:

❖ A deflated balloon

❖ A Pringles tube

PRANK PREPARATION:

⌘ Step 1: Take a full tube of Pringles, take the cap off and pull the film top back three quarters – do not pull this off completely

⌘ Step 2: Pour the Pringles out into a bowl. Place the deflated balloon into the Pringles tube. Pull the opening of the balloon over a tap and fill up to the top with water.

⌘ Step 3: Pull the opening of the balloon up to the rim of the Pringles tube. Pull the film over the top of the balloon and place the lid on trapping the opening of the balloon between the cap and rim. Use the pull tab on the film to cover the balloon.

⌘ Step 4: Wipe the tube down so that it's not wet then give the tube of Pringles to your target and wait for them to open the can and get soaked.

35. PEN CAP CAPER

Pull off this prank and when your target goes to use their pen to write that important note they are going to be met with nothing but rage and confusion.

PRANK RATING: Medium Mischief

MATERIALS:

- ❖ Your targets pen
- ❖ PVA Glue

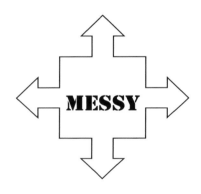

PRANK PREPARATION:

⌘ Step 1: Get hold of the pen you think your target might use.

⌘ Step 2: Half fill the cap of the pen with PVA glue.

⌘ Step 3: Put the pen into the cap tightly and leave to dry.

⌘ Step 4: When your target goes to use their pen they are going to wonder why they are suddenly so weak and can't open it.

⌘ Clean Up: PVA glue can be dissolved by placing the pen in hot water for a few minutes. Wipe with a cloth to dry.

36. ALARM CLOCK CHAOS

Pull off this prank and when your target goes to sleep they will be met with a rude awakening when a mysterious noise starts ringing out.

PRANK RATING: Medium Mischief

MATERIALS:

❖ An alarm clock

PRANK PREPARATION:

⌘ Step 1: Set an alarm clock or digital kitchen timer for an early time like 2am.

⌘ Step 2: Place the alarm clock underneath your targets bed in a place that isn't clearly visible.

⌘ Step 3: Go to sleep and wait for your target to be woken up in surprise when the alarm goes off. In the dark they will have to try and find where the noise is coming from to stop it.

37. IT NEVER RAINS IT POURS

Pull off this prank and when your target goes to open their umbrella they will be met with a very different kind of downpour.

PRANK RATING: *Medium Mischief*

ASK AN ADULT

MATERIALS:

❖ Your targets umbrella

❖ A newspaper

❖ A pair of scissors

MESSY

PRANK PREPARATION:

⌘ Step 1: Find your targets umbrella.

⌘ Step 2: Using a pair of scissors cut up a newspaper into small strips of newspaper.

⌘ Step 3: Open your targets umbrella and pour the torn up paper into the umbrella. Close up the umbrella, secure the fastener and place the umbrella back.

⌘ Step 4: Wait for the next time it rains and your target goes to open their umbrella and gets a different kind of shower.

38. TOILET ROLL TOMFOOLERY

Pull off this prank and when your target goes to wipe they are going to be met with quite a shock. Good job they are already sitting on the toilet!

PRANK RATING: Medium Mischief

MATERIALS:

❖ A marker pen

PRANK PREPARATION:

⌘ Step 1: Unroll a layer of toilet roll.

⌘ Step 2: Using the marker pen draw a large spider on the toilet roll.

⌘ Step 3: Carefully roll the toilet roll back up and wait for your target to go to the toilet and discover your hilarious handy work.

39. TOILET TERRORS

Pull off this prank and when your target goes to sit down on the toilet they are going to get a "cracking" surprise!

PRANK RATING: Medium Mischief

MATERIALS:

❖ Bangers – search fun snaps on Amazon

PRANK PREPARATION:

⌘ Step 1: Lift up the toilet seat. Place the bangers on the toilet rim in the position that the toilet seat rests when it is down.

⌘ Step 2: Gently lower the toilet seat down onto the rim so as to not set off the bangers.

⌘ Step 3: Wash your hands and then wait for your target to sit down on the toilet and get a rude awakening.

40. VARNISH VANDAL

Pull off this prank and when your target goes to use their pen or pencil they are going to be very confused when it just won't write like it used to

PRANK RATING: *Medium Mischief*

MATERIALS:

❖ Clear nail varnish

❖ Your targets pen or pencil

PRANK PREPARATION:

⌘ Step 1: Find your target's pen or pencil that you want to prank.

⌘ Step 2: Take the clear nail varnish and paint it over the tip of the pen or pencil. Allow this to dry and then repeat with two more coats.

⌘ Step 3: Wait for your target to try and use their pen or pencil and watch their frustration build.

⌘ Clean Up: The Nail varnish can be removed by using Nail Varnish remover.

HILARIOUSLY HARD

41. BALLOON LAMPOON

Pull off this prank and when your target goes to open their bedroom door they will be met with a wave of balloons.

PRANK RATING: Hilariously Hard

MATERIALS:

❖ Lots of balloons

❖ A balloon pump will help speed up the inflation process

PRANK PREPARATION:

⌘ Step 1: Wait till your target is either out of the house or going to be away from your target area for at least 30 minutes.

⌘ Step 2: Inflate the balloons and place them in your targets room.

⌘ Step 3: Wait for your target to open their door and be met with a tidal wave of balloons.

⌘ Alternative: If you do not have enough balloons to fill a room you could instead fill their wardrobe, drawers and cupboards with balloons instead.

42. SPONGE CAKE???

Pull off this prank and when your target goes to take a bite of a delicious slice of cake they are going to get a big mouthful of actual sponge.

PRANK RATING: Hilariously Hard

MATERIALS:

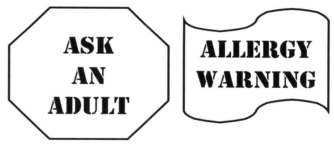

- ❖ A bath sponge
- ❖ A pair of scissors
- ❖ A mixing bowl, spoon, 125g Icing Sugar, 15ml of water and sprinkles to decorate

PRANK PREPARATION:

- ⌘ Step 1: Using a pair of scissors cut a bath sponge into small size squares.
- ⌘ Step 2: Mix up the icing sugar and water in a bowl to make a thick icing

⌘ Step 3: Spread the icing onto the pieces of sponge covering the top and sides and shake some sprinkles over the icing so it looks like a cake.

⌘ Step 4: Let the icing drive and then leave the cakes out on a plate for your target to find and take a bite.

43. FAMILY FORTUNES

Pull off this prank and your target will one day discover that all the photos in their house have been swapped for strangers.

PRANK RATING: Hilariously Hard

MATERIALS:

❖ Scissors

❖ Magazines with people in that you are allowed to cut up. Alternatively, you can print pictures off the internet.

❖ Photo frames

ASK AN ADULT

PRANK PREPARATION:

⌘ Step 1: Pick a photo frame that you want to prank. Carefully remove the photo from the frame making sure not to damage it, and place it in a safe place.

⌘ Step 2: Cut pictures out from the magazines to the right size to fit into the photo frame.

⌘ Step 3: Place these pictures in the photo frame, and close up the back of the photo frame

⌘ Step 4: Put the photo frame back in its original position making sure that it looks as normal as possible.

⌘ Step 5: Repeat for other photo frames and wait and see how long it takes your target to notice the change.

44. AMAZING APPLE

Pull off this prank and when your target goes to take a bite of apple they are going to find it to be a very hollow experience.

PRANK RATING: Hilariously Hard

MATERIALS:

- ❖ An apple
- ❖ A sharp knife
- ❖ A teaspoon

PRANK PREPARATION:

⌘ Step 1: With a knife cut a small chunk out of the bottom of the apple the width of a tea spoon. Keep this chunk in one piece and save for later.

⌘ Step 2: Using the knife and the teaspoon hollow out the inside of the apple without making the hole at the bottom any bigger. Make sure you don't break through the apple skin.

⌘ Step 3: When you have hollowed out the apple firmly push the bottom chunk back into the hole and wait for your target to take a bite.

45. CARWASH CAPERS

Pull off this prank and when your target goes to wash their car it's going to get very bubbly.

PRANK RATING: Hilariously Hard

MATERIALS:

❖ Washing up liquid or bath bubbles.

PRANK PREPARATION:

⌘ Step 1: Before your target goes to wash their car disconnect the hose connection where the water sprays out.

⌘ Step 2: Take your bottle of washing up liquid or bath bubbles and pour the whole bottle down into the hose.

⌘ Step 3: Re-attach the hose and wait for your target to turn on the water and start spraying foamy bubbles everywhere!

46. JELLY JOKES

Pull off this prank and when your target goes to wash their hands they are going to get a wobbly surprise.

PRANK RATING: Hilariously Hard

MATERIALS:

❖ An empty hand soap bottle
❖ Jelly powder

PRANK PREPARATION:

⌘ Step 1: Take an empty hand soap bottle. Unscrew the top.

⌘ Step 2: Pour in jelly powder and the required amount (see jelly packet) of water and gently shake.

⌘ Step 3: Screw the pump lid back on and place the bottle in the fridge for a few hours to let it set.

⌘ Step 4: Place the bottle in the bathroom and wait for your target to go and wash their hands boil with rage when the bottle is full but nothing comes out.

47. WATER BOTTLE WOE

Pull off this prank and when your target goes to pick up a bottle of water for a nice refreshing drink they are going to have a cold shower instead.

PRANK RATING: Hilariously Hard

MATERIALS:

- ❖ A sharp pointed knife
- ❖ A water bottle

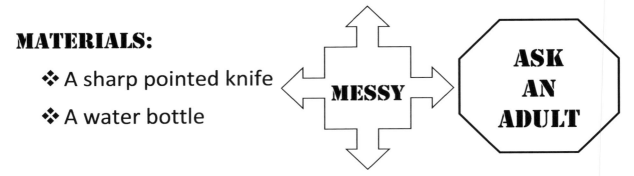

PRANK PREPARATION:

⌘ Step 1: Take an empty bottle of water, with a sharp knife poke lots of tiny holes in the bottom of the water bottle.

⌘ Step 2: Over a sink fill up the bottle with water and screw the lid on tightly. While the lid is on tightly the water won't come out.

⌘ Step 3: Wipe down the bottle with a cloth and then pass the bottle to your target.

⌘ Step 4: When they open the bottle the water will pour out of the holes in the bottle.

48. SHAVING FOAM SHENANIGANS

Pull off this prank and when your target goes to get out of bed they are going to get some seriously foamy feet.

PRANK RATING: Hilariously Hard

MATERIALS:

❖ Shaving foam

❖ Plastic bin bag

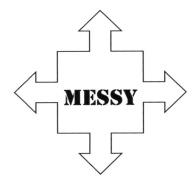

PRANK PREPARATION:

⌘ Step 1: Wait until your target has gone to sleep.

⌘ Step 2: In another room lay a plastic bin bag out flat and spray shaving foam over it.

⌘ Step 3: Sneak into your targets room and place the bin bag on the floor where your target will put their feet down when they get out of bed.

⌘ Step 4: Sneak out and wait for your target to wake up and get some foamy feet.

49. SUPER SPAM

Pull off this prank and your targets inbox will get flooded with tonnes of nuisance newsletters

PRANK RATING: Hilariously Hard

MATERIALS:

❖ Your targets email address

PRANK PREPARATION:

⌘ Step 1: Find out your targets email address.

⌘ Step 2: Go onto random websites like clothes stores and sign up for the company newsletter giving the email address of your target.

⌘ Step 3: Sign up for dozens of these and your targets inbox will soon be full of lots of random rubbish.

⌘ Clean Up: All of these newsletters can be unsubscribed from simply by clicking unsubscribe at the bottom of the email.

50. UPSIDE DOWN DAFTNESS

Pull off this prank and when your target goes into their room they will be confronted with a world the wrong way round.

PRANK RATING: Hilariously Hard

MATERIALS:

❖ No materials needed

PRANK PREPARATION:

⌘ Step 1: When your target is out of the house sneak into their room.

⌘ Step 2: Turn as many things as possible upside down – being careful not to break anything. If you are planning on turning heavy things like beds upside down, you may need a helper.

⌘ Step 3: Sneak back out and wait for your target to go into their room and discover their new interior design.

⌘ Clean Up: Make sure you help put the room back as it was after the prank has been played.

51. WATERFALL

Pull off this prank and your target will face an impossible puzzle of how to pick up an upside down glass of water.

PRANK RATING: Hilariously Hard

MATERIALS:

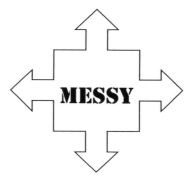

❖ A glass of water

❖ A thin piece of cardboard

PRANK PREPARATION:

⌘ Step 1: Half fill a glass with water and place a piece of cardboard over the top of the glass.

⌘ Step 2: Firmly holding the cardboard over the glass quickly turn the glass upside down and place on the kitchen countertop.

⌘ Step 3: Gently pushing down on the top of the glass quickly pull the cardboard out from under the glass. This needs to be done in one motion.

⌘ Step 4: Wipe up any water that may have leaked out.

⌘ Step: 5 Wait for your target to try and move the cup and send water everywhere.

⌘ Clean Up: Have a cloth or paper towels at the ready to help mop the water up.

52. PHONE FROLIC

Pull off this prank and your targets will think their precious mobile phone has been squashed by a giant.

PRANK RATING: Hilariously Hard

MATERIALS:

- ❖ Your targets phone
- ❖ A sheet of clear plastic and scissors
- ❖ A silver pen or silver paint.
- ❖ A ruler
- ❖ A pair of scissors

ASK AN ADULT

PRANK PREPARATION:

⌘ Step 1: Measure the size of your targets phone screen.

⌘ Step 2: Cut the plastic sheet to the right size to fit your targets phone screen.

⌘ Step 3: Using a silver pen or silver paint, draw a picture of a crack on the plastic sheet and wait for this to dry.

⌘ Step 4: When your target isn't looking place the plastic sheet over their phone screen so it looks like it has been cracked. Shout out "your phone is cracked" and wait!

53. DOOR DECEPTION

Pull off this prank and when your target enters the room they will be greeted with a shower of paper.

PRANK RATING: Hilariously Hard

MATERIALS:

- ❖ Newspaper
- ❖ Sellotape
- ❖ Scissors

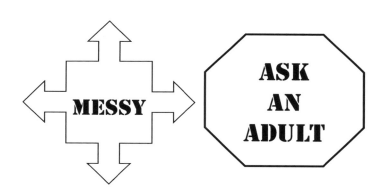

PRANK PREPARATION:

⌘ Step 1: Using a pair of scissors cut a newspaper into lots of small pieces.

⌘ Step 2: When your target is out of the room tape a sheet of newspaper from the top of the door to the wall over the door.

⌘ Step 3: Place the newspaper strips on top of the newspaper above the door. Call your target into the room and when they enter they will dislodge the newspaper and be covered in a shower of paper.

⌘ Clean Up: Use a dustpan to sweep up the mess and recycle the paper.

54. PENNY PUZZLE

Pull off this prank and your target will be left fuming that they can't pick up that shiny coin

PRANK RATING: Hilariously Hard

MATERIALS:

❖ A shiny coin – 50p, £1 or £2

❖ Superglue

PRANK PREPARATION:

⌘ Step 1: Find a suitably flat spot on the pavement outside your home.

⌘ Step 2: Take your shiny coin and carefully apply a large dollop of superglue onto one side of the coin.

⌘ Step 3: Without getting any glue on your hand, place the coin glue side down on the pavement.

⌘ Step 4: Firmly press down on the top of the coin and allow the glue to dry hard.

⌘ Step 5: Watch a passers-by fail one-by-one to pick up the coin.

55. MASH MADNESS

Pull off this prank and your target will be left wondering why instead of a nice cold mouthful of ice-cream they are stuck with a mouthful of mash.

PRANK RATING: Hilariously Hard

MATERIALS:

- ❖ A saucepan of water
- ❖ One large potato
- ❖ Potato peeler, knife, spoon and bowl
- ❖ A potato masher
- ❖ Chocolate Sauce and ice cream topping

PRANK PREPARATION:

- ⌘ Step 1: Peel and chop a large potato into chunks
- ⌘ Step 2: Place the potato in a saucepan full of water
- ⌘ Step 3: Boil Potato for 15 minutes on the hob. Be careful when handling hot water.

⌘ Step 4: Mash the potato. Once cool place in a bowl in the fridge for 30 minutes.

⌘ Step 5: Using a desert spoon scoop the mash into the shape of ice cream scoop and put in a bowl. Cover with toppings to hide the mash potato.

⌘ Step 6: Serve to your target and watch as they dig into a big bowl of mash!

56. EGGCELLENT IDEA 2

Pull off this prank and your target will be left bemused why they are so weak they cannot lift a single egg out of an egg box.

PRANK RATING: Hilariously Hard

MATERIALS:

❖ A box of eggs

❖ Superglue

❖ Newspaper

PRANK PREPARATION:

⌘ Step 1: Get a box of eggs and place them on a newspaper.

⌘ Step 2: Lift out each of the eggs and squirt in a dollop of super glue into the egg box.

⌘ Step 3: Place the egg in the box and press down gently.

⌘ Step 4: Wait for the glue to dry fixing the egg to the box.

⌘ Step 5: Leave the eggs on the side and wait for your target to try and make an omelette or scrambled egg!

57. WATER BOTTLE WASH

Pull off this prank and your target will be left soaked wondering how they managed to spill water all over themselves.

PRANK RATING: Hilariously Hard

MATERIALS:

- ❖ A disposable plastic water bottle
- ❖ A sharp knife

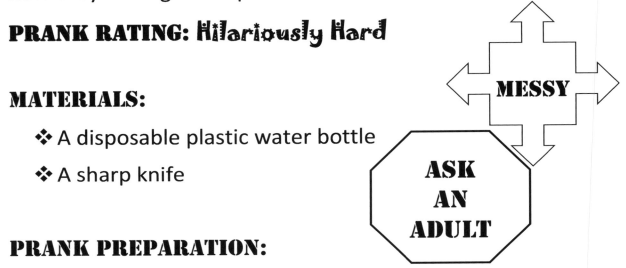

PRANK PREPARATION:

⌘ Step 1: Take the water bottle and fill it with water just below the top of the label

⌘ Step 2: Using a sharp knife make a few small holes in the side of the bottle just underneath the top of the label – make sure you make the holes above the level of the water and don't spoil the label.

⌘ Step 3: Pass the bottle to your target. When they go to drink the water they will get a soaking surprise.

58. BALANCING ACT

Pull off this prank and your target will be left balancing two cups of water with no option but to spill them.

PRANK RATING: Hilariously Hard

MATERIALS:

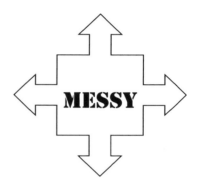

❖ Two plastic cups filled with water.

PRANK PREPARATION:

⌘ Step 1: Bet your target that they cannot hold out their hand palm down and balance a cup of water on it (they can do this sitting down or standing up). Make sure there are no electronics of valuable nearby.

⌘ Step 2: Once they agree place the cup of water on the back of their hand.

⌘ Step 3: When they successfully achieve this bet them that they can't do this with both hands. When they agree balance a second cup of water on their other hand. Once this is done your target will be trapped unable to either move or take the cups off their hands without spilling them.

59. WHY DOES MY SOAP SMELL LIKE CHEESE

Pull off this prank and your target will end up washing their hands with cheese and wondering why their hands smell like halloumi.

PRANK RATING: Hilariously Hard

ALLERGY WARNING

ASK AN ADULT

MATERIALS:

❖ A block of Halloumi cheese

❖ A knife

PRANK PREPARATION:

⌘ Step 1: Take a block of white cheese like Mozzarella or Halloumi out of their packaging. If necessary, cut the cheese so that it looks like the shape of a block of cheese.

⌘ Step 2: Place the cheese on the bathroom sink where the soap normally goes.

⌘ Step 3: Watch the bathroom carefully to see who goes in and ends up with stinky hands.

60. COOKIE MONSTER

Pull off this prank and when your target goes to bite into a freshly baked cookie they will get a very salty surprise.

PRANK RATING: Hilariously Hard

ALLERGY WARNING

MATERIALS:

❖ 225g butter, 350g salt, 275g plain flour and 225g butter

❖ Mixing Bowl, mixing spoon, baking tray

❖ Oven pre-heated to 190c

ASK AN ADULT

PRANK PREPARATION:

⌘ Step 1: Mix butter and salt until soft. Sift in flour and mix together. Get your hands in the bowl and knead the dough.

⌘ Step 2: Roll the dough into table tennis size balls and place them apart on a greased baking tray. When they are all spread out flatten them with the palm of your hand.

⌘ Step 3: Bake for 10 – 12 minutes

⌘ Step 4: Take out and allow to cool. When cool offer your target a fresh baked cookie and watch their face as they take their first bite.

<u>GRADUATION</u>

Congratulations......... if you have successfully pranked your way through all of this book then you have officially graduated from Prank Academy.

Over the course of the last 60 prank classes you have received a vigorous education in mischief, mayhem, tomfoolery and shenanigans.

The pranking doesn't end here though. If you are looking for more great pranks, follow us on Instagram **@theprankacademy** and feel free to share your ideas for your own practical jokes.

Printed in Great Britain
by Amazon